THE WORK of THE DEVIL

RED PENN

authorHOUSE

AuthorHouse™ UK
1663 Liberty Drive
Bloomington, IN 47403 USA
www.authorhouse.co.uk
Phone: 0800.197.4150

© 2017 Red Penn. All rights reserved.

No part of this book may be reproduced, stored in a retrieval system, or transmitted by any means without the written permission of the author.

Published by AuthorHouse 12/15/2016

ISBN: 978-1-5246-6217-2 (sc)
ISBN: 978-1-5246-6218-9 (e)

Print information available on the last page.

Any people depicted in stock imagery provided by Thinkstock are models, and such images are being used for illustrative purposes only.
Certain stock imagery © Thinkstock.

This book is printed on acid-free paper.

Because of the dynamic nature of the Internet, any web addresses or links contained in this book may have changed since publication and may no longer be valid. The views expressed in this work are solely those of the author and do not necessarily reflect the views of the publisher, and the publisher hereby disclaims any responsibility for them.

For my late friend Ben

CHAPTER 1

1:00 a.m.

It was a dark September night. The rain was falling heavily, and a strong gale whistled though the small, quiet town of Leighford, in the heart of America, swirling litter around the empty streets. It was a close-knit community where everybody knew each other, and news—or gossip—traveled fast.

Suddenly, a 1963 black Cadillac sped through the streets. The driver obviously knew this town very well (As he did some research online line, to try and find a quiet place to lay low) turning left then right to try to shake off the two deputies' cars that were chasing him with their sirens blaring and lights flashing.

All three cars were dented, and one of the squad cars only had one headlight working; the other had been smashed by the Cadillac. The front of the car and windscreen were splattered with mud, and it looked as though it had been involved in a long chase.

The Cadillac driver was six foot one, unshaven, in his early thirties, slim, and fit—like a man who exercised every morning—with dark-brown hair that was styled like James Dean. And on the back of his left hand, he had a medium-sized tattoo of a heart with an arrow passing through it. He was the biggest Shakespeare fan who used to drive his friends at work mad by quoting him whenever and wherever he could. He was wearing a red summer jacket and a white T-shirt like those worn in *Rebel without a Cause*.

One of the squad-car drivers, Michelle Matthews, was a white female from Santa Ana, California. In her early forties, she had straight, blonde hair, was slim, and stood five foot six.

Jack Stone was a white male in his early twenties. He was slim, five foot eight, and was from Oklahoma City, Oklahoma. The sheriff was a six-foot-two, well-built, tubby black male and with nice neat uniform, clean-shaven and always told pride in his appends, had lived in Leighford all his life. Today, he was celebrating his fortieth birthday, and he'd been a deputy sheriff in Leighford for the past fifteen years. He was a popular man, as he was very fair and professional when dealing with criminals.

All of a sudden, the first squad-car driver lost control as he turned a sharp corner, forcing him to crash sideways into some trees. As the other car drove past the deputy sheriff, Michelle Matthews turned her head to see if the two officers were injured. She watched one of the men clamber out of the car and pushed the accelerator pedal down hard, hitting the Cadillac's dented silver bumper just as the driver was lighting a cigarette with his lucky lighter. His girlfriend had bought it for him on their five-month anniversary, and she'd had his named carved on it. He dropped the lighted cigarette but found it before any damage was done and flicked it out of the slightly opened window.

THE WORK OF THE DEVIL

The Cadillac went speeding down the road, still being chased by the other car. A few shots were fired from the Cadillac, making the squad car swerve from left to right on the narrow country road. Without warning, a deer came from nowhere, causing Michelle to slam on her brakes and stop within inches of the animal. The deer just stood there and looked at her before heading back into the woods. Michelle took a deep breath, and the chase was on again.

She put her headlights on full beam and drove on for about another mile until she saw a car parked across the road. She stopped and got out of the squad car.

She walked over to the car, realizing that she could be in a dangerous situation, especially when she confirmed that the car was the Cadillac they had been chasing for hundreds of miles. Michelle peered into the car, which appeared to be empty.

Suddenly, Michelle heard a noise; she turned around slowly with her gun drawn, only to be blinded by the headlights of her own car. She raised her left hand to shield her eyes from the glare and thought she saw the silhouette of a man. She fired two perfectly aimed shots and heard a scream, but not from a man, as she'd expected. It was a woman's scream. There was a thud as the injured victim fell to the ground.

Michelle went to the squad car and turned the headlights down, and it was then that she realized that she had shot her younger sister, Katie. Katie had been in the Cadillac the whole time with her new boyfriend, who she didn't know was a wanted criminal in fourteen states.

Michelle went to her squad car and pulled out a first-aid box while dialing the emergency number for the paramedics on her cell phone—but it kept cutting out. She tried again, but nothing. She tried it one more time, but then the low-battery warning sounded. Why had she forgotten to charge it overnight?

By now, it had stopping raining.

Placing the first-aid box beside Katie, Michelle opened it and pulled out some bandages. She put the flashlight in her mouth so she had both hands free. Suddenly, she heard gunshots that made her jump and drop the flashlight.

She instructed her sister to keep the bandages pressed down hard and reassured her that she would get help as quickly as possible. Michelle snatched the flashlight from the road, pulled out her gun, and ran in the direction from where the gunshots had seemed to come.

Before she got to the other squad car, she saw Deputy Jack Stone lying still in the middle of the road. She called his name, but there was no response. She checked his airway, breathing, and circulation and realized that he was barely alive. Michelle said, "I'm gonna raise some help."

As the other officer was still in the squad car, she assumed that he must also be injured. She shined her flashlight on the deputy sheriff, but it was clear that it was too late for any help. He had been shot in the head at close range. The car radio had been trashed, so there was a moment's further delay before she reached her own car and was finally able to tell the sheriff's office about the seriousness of the situation and request backup. Michelle didn't notice that gasoline was dripping from the damaged car.

As Michelle was returning to Officer Stone to tell him that help was on the way, the Cadillac driver drew a cigarette from a battered packet, lit it, flicked it into the puddle of leaked gasoline, and walked away. The crashed squad car exploded, scattering debris over a wide area, and all Michelle could do was look on in disbelief.

She pulled herself together and, after realizing that she was in imminent danger, moved very carefully toward Katie while radioing the fire department. Katie had obviously overheard the message and was distressed, so Michelle stayed with her until the paramedics arrived some fifteen minutes later. Then she followed the ambulance with Katie inside.

Michelle wanted to be with Katie in the emergency room but was firmly asked to stay in the waiting area by a senior nurse. Thirteen minutes later, which seemed like thirteen hours, one of the ER doctors came into the waiting room and told her the bad news that Deputy Stone was dead. "We tried everything we could, but his injuries were very serious and he had lost a lot of blood. His internal organs were badly damaged."

"Shit!" Michelle said. "The bastard is gonna pay!" After a pause, Michelle took a deep breath and said, "Thanks, Doc. But what about the young lady? She's my kid sister."

Unfortunately, he couldn't tell her about Katie's condition, as she was being tended to in a different room by another emergency team.

At that moment, Katie was being wheeled out of the ER, and with long strides, Michelle caught up with Dr. John Carter to ask where his patient was going.

"She's on her way to the operating room," he replied.

Michelle followed along the corridor until they got to the operating room, where she prepared herself for another long stay in the waiting room. She was glad that the room was empty, as she wanted to be alone with her thoughts.

The receptionist said, "Nice weather today, isn't it?"

"Great," Michelle replied, and then she hid behind an out-of-date magazine that she had picked up from the metal table in the center of the room.

She flicked through the pages without seeing what was printed, just to pass the time, and before long, she fell asleep, as she was mentally and physically exhausted.

She awoke to see one of the nurses placing a welcome cup of coffee on the table. "I thought you might need this," she said with a smile.

Michelle looked at her watch. It was 4:23 a.m. She had slept for an hour. She said to the receptionist, "Please, may I use your phone?"

The receptionist showed her into an empty office and said, "You won't be disturbed or overheard in here."

Michelle updated the sheriff's office on the night's events.

After using the phone, she asked the receptionist if he had heard any news about a patient named Katie Matthews, but he hadn't, so Michelle went and sat back down. Then the OR doors opened, and out came Dr. Carter. Michelle leaped off her seat and walked toward him.

"I have some good news and some bad news," he said.

"What do you want first?"

"The bad," she said.

"Er ... erm ..." Dr. Carter cleared his throat. "Well, here goes. We did everything that we could, but—"

"Don't say it, Doc! Please, don't say it. She's isn't dead, is she?"

There were a few seconds of silence.

"No, you didn't let me finish. What I was going to say is that she's gonna have to stay in for a few weeks. We need to run some more tests and keep her situation monitored."

"Thank God; that's good news," Michelle replied.

"Yes, the good news is that she will make a full recovery for her wounds."

"Great, thanks, John; thanks again."

"Go home, Michelle, and get some rest. I'll let you know if there is any change in Katie's condition."

"Okay," said Michelle while looking for a piece of paper on which to write her cell and home phone numbers. She pulled a pen from the left-hand pocket of her blouse, scribbled down the numbers, and handed the paper to the receptionist so they could be added to Katie's records. Michelle left the hospital and was relieved to get into her car and drive home. She made herself a strong cup of coffee and then fed her cats—one was black and the other white—and went upstairs. She closed the curtains, took off her gun belt, and threw it on the wooden chair in the corner of her bedroom. She had just taken off her pants, when the phone rang.

"Damn it! Now what?" Michelle sighed. It was the sheriff's department. There had been another murder. "I'll be right there," she said, and within ten minutes of leaving her house, she was at the scene of the crime.

It seemed as though the whole sheriff's department was there, plus an ambulance, all with their lights flashing. She parked on the other side of the street, walked over to the crime scene, and asked a black deputy named Al Gibson, "What have we got here?"

"We have another murder on our hands. Take a look for yourself."

Michelle went into the house and saw a naked young lady about twenty years old lying in the middle of the room. Some of the furniture had been moved or broken, and it was evident that the young lady had put up a brave fight. The police had discovered that the victim's name was Susan, and she was alone in the house that night, as her husband was away on a business trip. Susan and her husband had only moved to the area a few weeks earlier, to get away from the big city of Los Angeles.

She had been severely beaten, resulting in bruises all over her body, and there were nine stab wounds in her chest. Two young deputies entered the room and immediately rushed out again with their hands over their mouths. One fainted just outside the door, and the other vomited.

"That's all we need," remarked Al as the body was being covered up. He walked over to Michelle and said, "You look beat. Go home. I'll let you know if we find anything new."

"Are you sure?"

"Yeah. Go; for God's sake, just go, and besides, I've just come on duty, and it looks like you've been on twenty hours."

Michelle left the crime scene at 6:23 a.m. and went straight home. This time, she got into bed and fell asleep. She was awakened at 7:32 by her cell phone ringing, and Michelle had put her phone on the charger, so she had to get out of bed and answered it. It was Doctor Carter, who said, "Katie is all right, and you can see her whenever you're free."

"Thanks, John. I will try and see her later today," Michelle replied. She was happy to know her younger sister would be all right. After feeding her cats and grabbing a piece of toast, her cell phone, some black coffee, and her house keys from the kitchen table, she made her way to the hospital. In her car, Michelle phoned to tell Dr. Carter that she was on her way and to ask if it was possible for him to meet her in reception. At the hospital, Michelle saw Carter arrive in the reception area just as she pushed open the glass door.

"Hi, John." John just gave a little smile. "Er … can I see her now and ask her any questions?" Michelle said.

"You can see her, but she has been through a lot these past days. Give her some time, please. Okay?"

"Yeah, sure, yeah … er … okay," Michelle replied.

"Shall we go and see her now?" asked John.

"Okay."

"Michelle, I've got something to tell you about Katie."

"What?" Michelle answered with a puzzled look.

"She's broken her left arm, but it is still well aligned, so it will almost heal itself."

"That's good news."

Katie's room was small and painted a dark blue, with a wooden door and two windows, one of which was letting in the outside world. It was a nice, peaceful view. The other window, its white blinds halfway down, enabled patients to see who was coming to visit them.

"Okay! Let's see how the one-armed bandit is doing."

Katie laughed. "He's been making jokes since they found out that I've broken by arm."

Dr. Carter looked at her charts and was satisfied with the observations that Katie was all right.

"I guess you two want to be alone for a while. I'll just get these forms filled out, and then I will be back to discharge you. You have been very lucky and recovered far quicker than I expected."

"Yeah, sure," said Katie.

When they were alone, Michelle started to ask questions. "Do you know the fugitive's real name? Where was he taking you? Did he give you any drugs?"

Katie just stared at Michelle for a few minutes saying nothing, and then she spoke in an angry voice. "What is it with all the questions? You didn't like me goin' out with someone diff'rent, did you?"

"I—" Michelle tried to finish her sentence when Katie butted in, saying, "I'm over twenty-one. I can date any guy I want, and I don't need to ask *you*!" Michelle started her sentence again.

"I just want you to be safe. You can help ID the stranger. He has, in fact, killed two sheriffs, and there has been another murder, but so far, we have found no evidence to link him with the young woman's murder. I just didn't want you to be victim number four."

"Sorry, I thought you were goin' all big sister on me and saying who I can and can't see."

CHAPTER 2

In the early hours of Monday, the stranger was packing a black sport bag, while Rita slept. Later that same day, the stranger drove up to his old school. He parked on the other side of the street, grabbed the sports bag, and walked over to the school, He went to the reception desk and asked the lady if he could see Mrs. Forbes.

"She's teaching," the young lady said.

"No matter, I'll wait. Er ... is there still a desk and wooden chair outside her room?" the stranger asked.

"Yeah."

"Is her room still 1B?" the stranger said.

"No, it's 2C. It will be a nice surprise for her to see one of her old students again after all these years," the receptionist said.

"Yeah, I think so," the stranger said. He walked to room 2C, put his sports bag on the table outside her room, pulled out two machine guns, loaded them, and strode into the classroom. All the children just looked at him, and then he said to Mrs. Forbes, "Remember me?"

Mrs. Forbes answered nervously. "No. I'm sorry, son; I'm afraid I don't."

"You kept puttin' me in detention for misbehaving in your class, and now I have come to give you and the kids 'ere what I've wanted to deliver to you, you 'orrible bitch, since the first lesson I had with you." And with that, he randomly fired at the whole class. "Revenge his foul and most unnatural murder," the stranger remarked, just note who's ever live. "A quote from Hamlet"

A male teacher from the opposite side of the hallway heard the noise and went in just as the stranger broke the window with a chair and was making his escape, leaving behind him a sea of blood and a hail of bullets.

A knife whizzed through the air toward the teacher and pierced his shoulder. If he hadn't been wearing his favorite thick tweed jacket, his injuries could have been much more serious.

Back at the house, Rita woke up just in time to see the stranger arrive back at home.

"Babe, today is a good day," he remarked.

"Why?"

"I've just sorted out my past."

He looked outside the window and could see people running toward the school. Police cars and ambulances were rushing by, their sirens blaring, in what seemed a real state of confusion. Someone shouted that there had been a brutal killing at the school. Rita joined the stranger at the window. She shuddered at what she saw, and when she glanced at the stranger, she noticed he was smiling. The truth then dawned on her. "Did you do that?" she asked. "Is that what you meant by 'sorting out your past?'"

The stranger turned around and, with his eyes open wide and still smiling, said, "That is what people get when they cross me!"

Rita was taken aback, thinking to herself that she would never forget that look or those words. She excused herself and went in to the toilet, where she was violently sick.

She was an absolutely terrified woman.

CHAPTER 3

Seventeen Months Earlier

One summery day at the end of April in North Carolina, a stranger was working at his desk when he received a message informing him that the boss wanted to see him in his office immediately. The stranger was told that his services were no longer required. He was given ten minutes to clear his desk and leave the building.

Later that day, around 5:00 p.m., the stranger was in his car when he saw his ex-boss walking toward the company limousine. The stranger opened his glove compartment and pulled out a gun to which a silencer had already been attached. He got out of the car and looked around to see if there was anyone around or if there were visible CCTV cameras about. There weren't. The coast appeared to be clear, so he walked up to his ex-boss and shot her three times in the chest. He ran to his car and sped out like a rocket. He drove through the night until he reached Virginia. He needed gas and to stretch his legs, so he pulled onto the forecourt of the next gas station. As he clambered out of the car, he was aware of a man and woman arguing but wasn't really interested in what was being said. He had enough problems of his own.

"Fill her up," he threw at the attendant as he made his way to the restroom. He freshened himself up a bit and returned to his car, stopping at the kiosk on the way to pay for his gas and purchase some gum. He was surprised to see that the lady, who had been arguing with someone when he'd arrived, was now alone and was loitering by his car.

"Want some company?" the lady said.

"Sure. Hop in."

"The name is Rita," she said. "And yours?" The stranger didn't answer her.

"Okay, fine. Don't tell, then," she remarked as they drove away, "but I shall have to call you something, or else I won't be able to think of you as a person, and then I won't speak to you."

The stranger started to talk. "What was all that about back there?"

"I hope I never see that fuckin' bastard again! Er … sure, I guess … er … he was stealing from me, and then I found out he was seeing another woman. I was devastated when I found out that the 'other woman' was a female whom I thought was my best friend."

That night, they slept in the car, waking up at about eight o'clock the following morning. They drifted through the next few days and nights together, and Rita was beginning to like this man who still had not divulged his name.

Conversation between them was still superficial, so although they talked a lot, they didn't really tell each other anything significant about themselves.

One morning, while they while driving along, but not particularly heading anywhere, they passed an abandoned, burned-out car. Rita divulged the fact that as a teenager, she had secretly wanted to steal good, quality cars, go joyriding, and then torch them. She admired the youngsters that carried out those crimes but used to feel that they underperformed, as they usually attacked cheaper cars. She still hadn't lost this yearning. Rita was surprised when the stranger expressed that he had had a similar dream. A look passed between them, and they both knew that the dream was going to become reality.

They excitedly made suggestions as to how they were going to carry out their plans. They knew that in spite of advice for motorists to lock their cars, many left them unlocked if they were only leaving the vehicle for a short time. They would also be able to steal saleable items from these cars before they set light to them.

They were in Kentucky when the strong feeling of revenge resurfaced in the stranger. For many years, he had felt the need to punish, in whatever way he felt appropriate at the time, any woman who reminded him, in any way, of the female teachers who had bullied, ridiculed, and humiliated him in his final years at that hateful school. His early school days had been quite happy, but that all changed when he reached puberty and had mature feelings for a particular attractive, young teacher. It was bad enough being rejected and to be told it was just a schoolboy crush, but he felt betrayed when he realized that the feelings that were so important to him had been laughed about in the staff room.

Rita had been safe in his company, as she didn't display any of the actions or characteristics that reminded him of those awful years. Also, over the last few weeks, he'd had some excitement in his life that had temporarily overshadowed his dark thoughts.

They were driving through one of the richer parts of Kentucky, both agreeing that some people lived a very expensive lifestyle and felt superior to those that were not so wealthy. The money they raised from the sale of items stolen from cars had allowed them to eat well, but now they wanted more.

It was about 11:00 p.m., and they decided that now would be a good time to break into one of those luxury homes. They chose one that was in all darkness, indicating that it was either empty or the occupants had retired for the night.

They broke in and were surprised how easily and quietly they gained access. There wasn't a dog on the premises, which was a relief. Neither of them were concerned about injuring humans, but an animal was another matter, even though they would not let one get in their way.

They quietly moved up the wide staircase—on creaky treads to announce their presence. Rita opened the first door, which revealed a tastefully furnished bedroom, but no occupants. "Only posh guests visit here," whispered Rita. "Lower-class bods like us will never be welcome by these filthy rich bastards."

The second door along the landing was open just enough for the stranger to see a young lady asleep on the bed. With two strides, he was beside her, and she stirred. He clasped his hand over her mouth.

"Don't scream; don't fuckin' scream and I'll let yer live," he said through clenched teeth.

Rita had been looking in the other rooms. "There's a couple of old wrinkles in the next room—'spect they're 'er parents."

"Excellent!" he remarked and proceeded to coldly rape the girl while Rita watched, totally without emotion.

As they were leaving, the stranger turned to the sobbing girl and said, "Daddy can't protect you all the time, you damn bitch, but I bet he'll make sure you have the best treatment that money can buy if you need an abortion, so all's well that ends well."

The following night, they visited the upmarket area of Kentucky and broke into a couple of expensive homes. The first residence was unoccupied, so the stranger did not get the thrill he wanted. He was luckier in the second house and was able to perform the action that always gave him the most excitement. He viciously raped the young girl in her own bed. As he reached the door, he said, "To be or not to be. That is the question. Whether it is better to be raped or end up a frigid old virgin!"

Rita just laughed and felt pleased that the stranger allowed her to accompany him. Having her as a spectator certainly didn't seem to affect his performance.

They laid low for a few weeks and had moved onto Illinois. There had been no excitement in their lives, and they were both very bored. "Time for a bit of kick," said Rita. "I'm fed up with keepin' within the law most of the time. It's so dull."

"I feel that way myself. Tonight's the night."

As night fell, they drove around until they saw a house that caught their fancy. They parked on the opposite side of the street, and the pair clambered out of the car. They walked up the path to the front door, feeling the adrenaline rush—a feeling that they both enjoyed and needed. As they reached the door, it was opened by a young man of medium height and build. "Yes! Can I help you?"

"Yeah," the stranger replied. "Our cell phones are dead. Could we use your landline?"

"Er ... I guess so," said the young man and stepped aside to let them in. Rita extended her hand, indicating that the young man should go first. They entered the hall and the stranger closed the street door behind them, at the same time pulling his gun from an inside pocket. Rita already had her firearm at the ready.

"Get in the living room," Rita snarled.

The terrified man hesitated, as he feared for his family, but was brutally pushed through the door into the room where his wife was reading a story to her two children.

"Sit down!" shouted Rita.

"What do you want?" asked the wife.

"Silence!" Rita screamed as she fired a shot, hitting the young man in his left shoulder.

"You bastard! Get out of my house!"

"Shut your fuckin' mouth before I shut it for you permanently!" growled the stranger, hitting him with a heavy vase on his injured shoulder.

"We don't have much money," wept the wife, but she was interrupted by the grinning stranger, who stated that they didn't want their damn money. The mission was just to torture the family—very slowly. He then hit her several times across the face, splitting her nose and lips.

"Stop that!" cried one of the children.

"Well, well, what do we have here? Fucking Superman?"

"Don't hurt him," pleaded the father.

"Why not? Don't see why he shouldn't be included in our fun."

"My husband needs to get to the hospital," the wife said, ripping the sleeve from her blouse to put on the wound.

"Ha! Fat chance," the stranger said, pointing the gun at him. "I could save you the time and effect by killin' him right now; then you wouldn't need a doctor."

"You bastard!" the wife said.

"Mummy, Mummy, what's wrong with Daddy?" one of the children said.

"It's okay, babe. Daddy will be fine; you'll see."

"Ah, that's so sweet, lying to your own kids," Rita interjected.

"What does she mean, Mummy? You said lying is naughty," sobbed the frightened child.

But the mother didn't answer, as she was now only too aware that her husband was slipping in and out of consciousness. She ripped the other sleeve from her blouse to apply more pressure on the wound, which was still bleeding heavily.

"Hang in there, darling," the wife said as she started to cry.

By this time, the stranger was getting impatient. He pointed his gun at the injured man, finger on the trigger.

"No! Don't shoot!" yelled the wife, wiping the tears from her eyes. "Kill me, but let my husband live."

Rita looked admiringly at the stranger as he said sarcastically, "He's in a worse state than you are. He's dying. Surely you want me to put him out of his pain."

"No," the wife said. "Look, I have a plan. You go, and I will just call the hospital—no police, just an ambulance."

"You're crazy if you think that we are that dumb. He's lost a lot of blood, so do you really think that in about ten or fifteen minutes, he'll still be alive? He'll snuff it while waitin' for help to arrive," the stranger said. "If you want your husband to live and for us to get out of your home, you're going to have to kiss my girlfriend."

Rita looked at the stranger and then at the wife. "Sure thing. I'm up for that," she said.

"I'm not doing that," the wife said through clenched teeth.

The husband managed to whisper, "Do it if it gets these punks out of my house."

"No. That is just sick," the wife replied.

"Then your husband will die in front of you, and you will always remember that you may have been able to save him. Your children will grow up not knowing their father. It's your choice. Well, what's your answer?" the stranger said. "Shut up, kids!" he shrieked.

The stranger asked where the power tools were kept, and the wife said that she didn't know. He delivered a sharp blow across her mouth and told her to stop lying. With blood running from her mouth, she told him that they were kept in the basement.

Telling Rita to keep them covered with the gun, he ran downstairs and quickly returned with a fully charged cordless power drill. He grabbed the older child and started to drill through her foot.

"Stop that! Okay, let's get this over with, if it will get you two out of this house."

The wife got up from the floor, and the stranger sat down on the sofa so the two women could kiss.

"Thank you, ladies," the stranger said and was then immediately surprised when Rita shot the husband in the chest.

"No!" the wife screamed.

"Let's get out of here, babe," Rita said. They made a hasty exit.

"What was all that back there?" queried the stranger.

"He would never have forgiven his wife for kissing another woman. He only wanted her to go through with it for his benefit, so I've saved her from the beating."

"We need to get out of this state. Where would you like to go next?" the stranger asked.

"I've heard that Missouri is nice this time of year."

After being stuck in heavy traffic, they finally arrived there later that evening. They pulled into a gas station to fill up. Rita told the stranger to wait in the car for her and she would be back in a moment. He thought she seemed edgy but didn't take a lot of notice.

"Where have you been?" the stranger asked on her return.

"The ladies' room," she said.

In fact, she had just killed the gas station attendant and dragged his body into the men's room, all because she had been annoyed by the way he looked at her and told her she had a nice ass. She thought she deserved more respect.

They found a cheap motel and spent the night there. The next morning, Rita woke up early. She decided to get some breakfast from town. When she returned, the stranger was awake, and he let her in. She put the bags of food on the counter and then went back outside to lock the car. Back inside, she shut the motel door behind her and gave the stranger a look that he was beginning to know well.

"Are you crazy? It's six o'clock."

"Come on, babe," Rita said.

She pushed the stranger onto the bed and she took off her top. Then she removed the stranger's T-shirt and then his boxers. As she took off her jeans and underwear, the stranger realized that he was really aroused and that it didn't matter what time of the day it was. She climbed on top of him and he started feeling her body and her breasts, and then they kissed. The earth moved for both of them. She fell asleep in his arms.

Rita awoke first and turned on the TV. The reporter was saying that a body had been found in the men's room at a gas station. The police said there was not much evidence to go on at this time but they were sure they would bring the man responsible to justice, in due course.

Rita was happy about that. At least they weren't looking for a woman. She switched off the TV and woke up the stranger for some breakfast, and then they moved on.

New Year's Eve rolled around. The stranger and Rita didn't want to celebrate; instead, they wanted an early night in a nice, comfortable bed. They broke into an elegant-looking house that satisfied their needs and fell asleep around 11:00.

The stranger was awoken at 1:00 a.m. by very loud music. It was coming from next door. The front door was open, so he walked in, approached a group of teenagers, and inquired who was running the party.

"Joe is," replied one of the lads.

"Where can I find this Joe?" the stranger said.

"Over there," one of the teenage girls said, pointing to Joe.

The stranger walked over to Joe. "Could you turn the music down, please?"

"No way, man," another of Joe's friends said. "It's New Year's Eve, after all, a good excuse for a party. Everybody should be celebrating."

"Who do you think you are crashin' my party?" Joe said.

"Just turn it down. I've had a bad week!" the stranger shouted. No one took notice of his request. The stranger went to the car and pulled a blanket from the truck. He walked back into the house where the rowdy party was going on.

"You're back, man!" Joe said, pulling out a knife.

"Yeah, what are you gonna do about that, *man*?"

"Leave, man, or I will stick this in you!" Joe said, his hand shaking.

"Try it, kid," the stranger said, removing the blanket to reveal a machine gun.

"Hey, it's cool, man. Turn the music off, Sarah," Joe said. "What the hell, man?"

"No, turn the music up. I want all you kids to have fun. Turn it up!" said the stranger.

"What? Just do it," Joe said and nodded to another teenager who was by the stereo, and she turned it up. The stranger shot all the revelers, the last shot fired at the stereo. Silence at last.

"Happy New Year, motherfucker."

He returned to the house they had broken into and was surprised to discover that Rita was still sleeping, undisturbed by all the noise.

After months of drifting from town to town and leaving behind them a world of tortured and murdered victims, they picked up a young girl in Idaho named Katie.

Katie eagerly participated in the crime with Rita and the stranger. The three of them were on the highway to Leighford when they were stopped by the local deputy sheriff pulling up in front of them.

Michelle got out of her car, walked over to the black Cadillac, and switched on her flashlight, which she shined at the driver only.

"Can I see your license and registration, please, sir? Do you know why I stopped you?" Michelle said.

The stranger handed over his license and registration and said, "What's the problem, Officer?"

"You have a broken taillight."

"I didn't know that, Officer. It must have been some kids."

Michelle walked toward her car to check the documents, but before she reached it, the black Cadillac sped off, tires screeching. Michelle radioed for backup.

CHAPTER 4

Present Day

The stranger and Rita were in yet another motel. They were talking about what they would do if ever they won the largest prizes in the lottery. They both agreed that those people who thought that the top money prize should be reduced and more punters given a chance to win something must be very dull and had no sense of adventure. If that was how they felt, then they shouldn't win at all.

The stranger had dreamed of having such a large sum of money at his disposal, and since his reign of terror had started, he had been studying the layout and procedure of many banks. He realized that there were flaws in the security, and some of them seemed to lack well-practiced safety procedures for the staff and customers. He told Rita that he was interested in the bank in town.

"So?" Rita said.

"So! What do you mean, 'so?' Come on, babe! You're not looking at the whole picture. Let's rob it."

Rita looked puzzled. "You're joking, ain't you? How long have you been planning to do this job?"

"I've been thinking about it for a long time. I just needed to know that I could really trust you to be my accomplice. I think you passed your probationary period with flying colors," he said, giving her left cheek a friendly tweak.

"I think that the best time will be next Friday night … er … I just need a few more days to check out the security system and confirm how many security men are in the bank. I think I know the answer to that, but I want to be sure. The men I have seen seem to be more interested in eyeing up the pretty customers than any security measures. That's where you may be useful if we have to change our plans and carry out the exercise during opening hours."

"You're serious?" Rita said.

The stranger made several trips into town over the next few days, making mental notes, and he decided that the day and time he had originally planned was right.

On Friday night, they were ready to put their plan into action. The adrenaline was flowing. They pulled into the unfinished cul-de-sac at the back of the bank and turned the car around so that it would be facing the right direction when they wanted to make their getaway. The stranger removed a sports bag from the trunk.

"Are you sure that there are only two security guards doin' the night shift?"

"Yes, babe, and I expect they take it in turns to sleep, if the truth is known. Don't you trust me? I hope you aren't gettin' cold feet, as I need your full cooperation," the stranger said.

"Yeah, I trust you. Can we get on with the job?" Rita replied.

"Fine by me!"

There was some building work being carried out that entailed the alarm system being temporarily disconnected. The average customer would not have noticed, but the stranger spotted that one tiny light was not illuminated. He knew a bit about security alarms and was able to find the information he wanted on the Internet. The alarm was not active.

They silently broke the grass in a small side window and entered the dimly lit room. When he was checking out the place, the stranger had wondered why the powers that be had not considered it necessary to fit toughened glass into that window, but he was glad they hadn't done so. He handed a knife to Rita and put his fingers to his lips. They listened and were aware of approaching footsteps. Rita realized that it was the security guard doing his rounds. They flattened themselves against the wall and held their breath. The guard turned around just before he reached them and Rita stepped out and threw the knife, hitting the guard in the back. He slumped to the floor.

"Excellent work! Where did you learn that trick? Were you in a circus?" the stranger asked. "But don't kill the other one; we need him to open the vault."

"But won't it be on some sort of timer?" she asked.

"No!"

They heard something, so they went and hid in an office. It was the other security guard.

"Hey, Frank! The game's about to start!"

As there was no reply, the guard assumed that his partner was in the bathroom and would soon be joining him in front of the television to watch what they hoped would be an exciting game.

Rita and the stranger moved to where the guard was glued to the television screen.

"Come on, Frank. This already looks as though it is going to be a hard-fought game. Good thing we both support the same team, buddy. Where were you? It's not like you to miss the beginning of a match."

"Think again, chummy!" Rita said. "I am not your fuckin' mate."

"Where's Frank?"

"Never mind him! Just get your backside off that chair and open up the vault," hissed the stranger.

"No way, man. I'm only a guard here, not the bank manager. He and the assistant manager are the only ones with access to the vault," the security guard replied, slowly pulling out his gun. "Can't help you."

The stranger looked at Rita and pulled out a machine gun. "Maybe this might change your mind. We know that the alarm system is not fully operational at the moment. The bank staff should be careful as to who is listening when they talk about problems with the security system. The time-lock can be overridden, and you know how to do that, so get moving if you don't want to be turned into a colander. Drop your gun, *now*," the stranger said as he raised the machine gun.

"Okay, whatever you say, man," the security guard said in a trembling voice as he let his gun slide to the floor.

They walked in single file along a narrow passage, and the vault surprisingly opened without too much effort. The stranger could not believe that a small bank such as this carried so much money, especially when the alarm system was faulty. He thought that the bank manager should have arranged for some of the bills to be stored in another branch, but he was glad that hadn't been done. This was going to be easier and more profitable than he had ever dreamed. The stranger told Rita to keep the guard covered and not to hesitate to kill him if he tried something clever, like moving. He then began stuffing black bags with wads of used bills of all denominations.

"Can't I kill the bastard right now?" she said.

"No! He's more useful to us alive!"

"Why?" she said.

"May need a hostage," the stranger said. "I've nearly finished here, so get him back to the office and keep him covered. We'll bind and gag him."

As they reached the office, Rita tripped. In the split second when she glanced down at the floor to see what had caused her to trip, the security guard was able to press the panic button, which was connected to the local sheriff's office, without being noticed.

Rita saw the security guard glancing toward the window and almost immediately heard sirens. She guessed what had happened and was happy that the sheriff was stupid enough to have the sirens working, as that had given her some warning. She fired a shot at the security guard.

"Let's get out of here! Come on!" she said as she grabbed as many sacks as possible. An unexpected shot rang out as the stranger struggled with the rest of the bags. The dying guard had summoned enough strength to shoot the stranger in the leg before taking his last breath.

"Motherfucker ... Rita, help! I've been fucking shot!"

"Hang in there. I'll be back in a minute." She shoved the sacks into the car. She could hear the sirens getting nearer. She was grateful that sound carried a long way in this area on a quiet night. It gave them a few extra vital minutes. Rita ran back to the stranger, grabbed the sacks and the sports bag, and went back outside. Then she saw the sheriff's car pull up. *Shit! Damn it!* she thought as she hid inside the car.

Inside the bank, the stranger tried to escape through the window he had entered through but was hampered by his wounded leg. One of the deputies called for the coroner and an ambulance, while Melissa stopped the stranger from making his escape.

"Freeze!" Deputy Melissa shouted, pointing her gun at his head.

"Crap," the stranger said.

"You're under arrest. Turn around! Turn around, or I will shoot!"

The stranger obeyed. He liked to put up a fight but wasn't ready yet to commit suicide.

"Oh, God, we need to get you to a hospital," Melissa said as she was cuffing him.

Outside, Rita watched from the car and saw a deputy and the stranger entering the ambulance. When she thought it was safe to do so, she drove to the hospital. Rita parked the car in the entrance, entered the emergency room reception area, and asked the receptionist if a tall man with a leg injury had been brought in by a deputy.

"Yes. He's with the doctor now."

"Thanks," Rita said.

She went into the doctor's lounge and removed a white coat that was hanging on the back of the door. *Phew! That was easy*, she thought. *These doctors are so careless. I thought these coats would be in lockers to stop people like me getting hold of them.*

She quietly laughed to herself as she looked at the schedule. "Mr. X, leg injury" was entered under Examination Room 3.

So they don't know his name either, she thought.

Rita looked into the room and saw him cuffed to the bed. There was not a deputy in sight; just two nurses and a doctor were attending to him.

"This patient must be moved immediately. This room is needed."

"And you are?" the doctor said.

"Er ... right ... yes, sorry, I should have introduced myself. Er... I'm Doctor Lapper. It's my first day here. We've got casualties from R.T.A. on the way. ETA about ten minutes."

"Okay, let's move him," one of the nurses said and then told the other nurse to report the pending move to the deputy.

"Don't you worry about that; I'll explain it to him myself," Rita said.

"Her!" corrected the nurse.

Rita and the nurse pushed the trolley into a smaller cubicle. "Thanks," Rita said.

"We've got a few minutes before R.T.A. is due. Why don't you and your colleague go and get yourselves a drink. You never know when you may get other opportunity today."

"Are you sure? Thanks," the nurse said as she was leaving. She wished that there were a few more considerate doctors like Dr. Lapper. She thought that she would like working with her.

"Hi, babe. Am I glad to see you. I thought you had forgotten me and done a runner with the money," the stranger whispered. "Could you get these damn cuffs off?"

Rita checked the cuffs and was pleased to see that they were the old type that could be picked without too much difficulty. It was amazing what she could do with a hair clip and a nail file.

"How's the leg?" Rita asked as she moved a wheelchair alongside the hospital bed.

"Good as new. The bullet had not gone in very deep, so they were able to remove it under a local anesthetic. I was really lucky. It entered the thickest part of my thigh but missed major blood vessels. I heard the doctor say that if it had hit the femoral artery, things would have been a lot different." Rita quickly removed the doctor's coat, put it in the soiled linen bin and covered it with used bed linen, and then pushed the wheelchair and its occupant to the car.

Meanwhile, Deputy Melissa returned to the room where she had last seen Mr. X. "Oh! You're back. Where have you been?" the doctor said, rather angrily, as he didn't like being left with a patient who was in police custody.

"It was police business. I had to report your findings and tell my boss when we would be leaving here … what the … where's the patient?" Melissa asked.

"Doctor Lapper took him to another room."

"I'll show you where he is," the nurse said as she returned from having a welcome cup of coffee.

She pushed open the door of the small cubicle farther along the corridor, but the room was empty. She noticed that there was linen in the bin, which was surprising, as she had seen it emptied only half an hour ago and the room had not been used before Mr. X was moved there. She tipped out the contents and found the discarded white doctor's coat.

"I had a feeling about that doctor," the nurse said. "Usually, you get to hear if a new doctor is starting, and someone shows them around and points out where vital pieces of equipment are sited."

Melissa reported the escape to the sheriff's office.

The stranger and Rita arrived back at the motel. Rita helped the invalid into their room and returned to the car to remove the sacks from the trunk, making sure that she was not observed. They were like children on Christmas morning when they started counting the money.

"We've hit the jackpot!" the stranger exclaimed.

"What are we gonna do with it? We can't put it in the bank. Someone might steal it." Rita laughed.

CHAPTER 5

Michelle had been in the office all morning, writing reports, reading the coroner's reports, and trying to figure out how all these events tied up with the death of her two friends and how Katie had come into it all.

After hours in the office, Michelle needed to clear her head and think things out. She wanted fresh air and a walk. She informed the duty officer were she was going and told him that if anything came up, she could be contacted on her cell phone.

Michelle wandered around the town as she had done so many times before, but this afternoon was different. She found herself near the old high school, and she gazed at the playground where she and Katie once played. Memories from the Sixties came flooding back to her.

Michelle was two years older than Katie. It was Michelle who was the driving force behind her little sister. It was Michelle who was always making sure that Katie did her homework. In other words, it was Michelle that kept Katie on the straight and narrow. She loved her little sister so much.

According to their father, Michelle had all the brains. Without thinking, he had said as much in front of Katie, who became a little jealous of Michelle. The jealousy grew. The more Michelle achieved, the more jealous Katie became. The final straw was when Michelle won a scholarship so she could go to college and then on to the police academy. Katie couldn't accept that was what Michelle wanted and had worked hard for it. She felt that Michelle got everything she wanted and it just wasn't fair.

When the day arrived for Michelle to leave for college, Katie made it quite clear that she was going to have a life of her own. She wasn't going to spend time with her nose stuck in books when she could be having fun. Katie didn't stay around to say good-bye and wish her big sister luck. Michelle was very hurt.

College life for Michelle was hard going. She had a part-time job to pay for her rent, books, and food, as they didn't come cheap, but all in all, she was enjoying herself and studying hard.

Michelle tried to go back to Leighford as often as she could. Katie was seldom at home when Michelle made these visits, and if she was there, she would just stay in her bedroom. If Michelle tried to talk to her, they always argued, and it ended by Katie walking out of the house and returning very late. What was happening to her little sister?

When final exams were over, Michelle came home for a few weeks before joining the academy. The rift between Michelle and Katie was now even greater. They hardly spoke to each other. Dad was being kept busy at the sheriff's department because of staff shortage, so he couldn't keep an eye on Katie, who, by now, was being a real problem. Their mother had inoperable lung cancer, and it wasn't known how long she had to live—maybe weeks, maybe months, or, if she was lucky, it could be a year. She had been a heavy smoker since she was a teenager and for some months had been in the hospital more than she had been at home. She hadn't listened to the doctors' warnings over the years, and now the nicotine had taken its toll. Katie was left to her own devices and mixed with some bad company. Dad tried to keep some sort of control over Katie, but the stress of work and looking after his wife didn't leave him with much energy to cope with a wayward daughter.

Ten months into the academy training, which was in the Vietnam era, Michelle got a telegram saying that possibly her mother had only a few hours to live, therefore she should return home immediately.

Michelle arrived home early the next morning, but she was too late. Her mother had died during the night. Michelle found her dad all alone in the house. He had always been a strong man, but now he looked lost and frail. Katie was nowhere to be found. Dad told Michelle that something else had cropped up. He had been a reserve for the marines for many years and had been called up for a tour of duty in two weeks' time. He hadn't been called up for a while, and although he could probably be excused on compassionate grounds, he felt that it would take his mind off things.

Somehow, Katie had found out when her mother's funeral was taking place and turned up for the service, much to the relief of Michelle and her father. They had hoped to speak with her, but she was nowhere to be seen when the ceremony was over.

Katie had stepped out of their lives again. Michelle knew that her father hadn't the time or the inclination to look for her. He was distressed by his wife's death and was also trying to prepare himself mentally for the forthcoming tour of duty. Michelle was staying with her father for a few days and just hoped that Katie would come to her senses and come back home while she was there.

Katie did finally return and looked like death warmed over, which caused her father and sister to worry even more.

The week following the funeral was a busy time. Michelle went with her dad to see a lawyer regarding her mother's will. The little that her mother had, had all been left to her father. While they were at the lawyer's office, Michelle's father updated his will, knowing that he was going to Vietnam soon.

Once the business with the lawyer was completed, they moved on to the sheriff's office. It felt strange for Michelle's dad to be clearing the desk he had occupied for so long and to hand the keys over for his successor. Under normal circumstances, Jack, his deputy, would have taken over from him, but he had also been called up to serve in the same unit as Michelle's father, so the post was currently vacant. He didn't know if he would have the same position when he returned, but that seemed unimportant at the time.

Michelle promised her father that she would continue to work hard at the academy and hoped that one day, she would be in this department and if allowed, they would travel on their rounds together. They looked at each other and shared a hug.

How different my two daughters are, he thought. He handed over his badge, gun, and the rest of the paraphernalia, had a nostalgic look around, and left the building. Michelle was lucky to be able to have two weeks' vacation attached to her compassionate leave. The time passed by so quickly, as there was so much to do. The furnished house went with the job, so it had to be vacated in readiness for the new sheriff. They sold the few extras that had accumulated over the years and put the proceeds into an account for Katie to keep her going for a while until she was on her feet. Their father would have to find new accommodations when he returned. They managed to find a small apartment for Katie and a job for her at the local diner.

The time soon came for Michelle and Katie's father to leave to join his unit in Vietnam. Katie refused to go with her father to the train station. She gave him an unexpected kiss and a hug and closed the door to her room. Michelle drove her father to the station in their old Jeep. The parting was emotional for both of them. He had only been called up for short periods before, but this time, he could be away for a couple of years. "I'm doing this for my country," he said.

Katie packed her things and moved into her apartment. Michelle was due to leave the following day to return to the academy. The sisters said their good-byes, and Michelle felt as though their relationship was a little happier. Katie promised Michelle that she would keep her job and she would write to let her know how she was coping.

Michelle received a letter from her father saying that he and Jack were fine. They were hoping that they would not have to be shipped out and that they would be able to stay in their base and be put on the training squad. He may then be able to get leave to visit his two girls. If he was shipped out, he would not be able to let her know before they left, so not to worry if she didn't hear from him for a time. They never had that visit. Michelle would never see her father again.

Katie wrote for a while, as promised. Michelle was studying for her final exam at the academy, so she hadn't had a letter from her sister for a while. It had also been quite a time since Michelle had written, as she usually answered letters, but there hadn't been any to answer. Michelle wrote daily over the next week, but the letters were returned unopened and marked "Not known." She knew she had to return to her hometown soon to see if she could find out what had happened to her sister.

At the first opportunity, Michelle made her way to Leighford. She went straight to her sister's apartment and found it empty. There was no forwarding address left in the mailbox. She then called in at the diner but was told that Katie had not reported for work for some weeks and they had not heard anything from her. The sheriff's office was her next port of call, and she introduced herself to the new sheriff. Michelle asked him, "Has Katie Matthews left a forwarding address?"

"No," he replied.

The only news he was able to give Michelle about Katie was that one of the deputies had picked her up for being drunk.

Michelle was about to leave when the sheriff asked her to step into his office. She was surprised to see another person in the office. It was a man whom she had grown up with. He was a bit older than her, and they had been good friends but not serious enough to keep in touch. He was now a deputy. When Michelle was seated, the sheriff handed her an envelope, which she opened nervously. It contained the telegram she had been dreading, together with her father's dog tag. The telegram stated that Sergeant Matthew G. Matthews had been killed in action. She brushed a tear from her eye and thanked the sheriff for allowing her some privacy. She asked why the telegram had been sent to them instead of her and was told that had been at her father's request. He knew that her old friend had been appointed as a deputy in the old town, and he thought it would be kinder if he could give her any bad news instead of her receiving it in an impersonal way. The sheriff had arranged for the deputy to have some time off to deliver the telegram, but Michelle had turned up at the office instead.

The sheriff asked Michelle how she was getting on at the academy and asked when she would finish her training. He informed her that he had had the honor of meeting her father a few years prior and had respect for the man. He also told her that her father had had a very good reputation and told his colleagues that he would be very proud if one day his daughter could work with him in this department. Unfortunately, this would never be the case, but if she wanted, she could be employed in this department as a deputy. Michelle thanked the sheriff for the offer but explained that she wanted to get things sorted out first. If he would leave the offer open, she would give him an answer once she had sorted out her father's business and done everything she could possibly do to find her sister.

The sheriff agreed that she had to get her priorities right and that in the meantime, he would make inquiries locally and in surrounding counties to find out if anyone had any news about Katie. He promised that if he received any information, he would pass it on to Michelle immediately.

Michelle thanked him and then made her way to the lawyer's office, which was now being run by the son. The father had been semi-retired for a few years, as he had decided that it was the right time to leave the business in his son's capable hands while he was still around to give advice but active enough to enjoys some of his hobbies and have a few well-earned holidays with his wife. Fortunately, there wasn't a lot for

Michelle to do, as her father's will was quite straightforward, as was his life insurance.

    After receiving her very good results a few days later, Michelle cleared her room at the academy and moved into her sister's apartment. She unloaded her few possessions and then went to the sheriff's office to find out if the offer was still open. Fortunately, it was, and it was agreed that she would be sworn in and commence duties on the following Monday.

CHAPTER 6

Quite often, after a stressful shift, Michelle liked to stroll around a park in the center of town. There was a small cenotaph in memory of the local men who had fallen in the Vietnam War. On this day, she was extremely tired, so she sat on one of the beaches just inside the gates instead of walking all round the perimeter as usual. As she sat there, she heard a familiar voice. It was Jack, her father's old deputy. Jack used to walk around the town and through the park with her father. Jack was now blind from the same bomb blast that had killed her father.

Jack said farewell to the lady he was speaking with and walked toward the bench where Michelle was sitting. She watched him as he tap, tap, tapped his way along. She thought how tragic it was to see this once very active man finding his way around with a white stick, but she also admired him for the way he was coping with the disability.

"Hello, Jack," Michelle said. Jack smiled and then sat beside Michelle and put his arm around her. She rested her head on his shoulder.

"Do you miss him, girl?"

"Oh, yes, I do! I miss him, all right. More than I thought possible."

Michelle and Jack walked out of the park. It was getting dark and the streetlights were coming on. Michelle wondered if Jack realized that this was happening.

Michelle left Jack outside the "old soldier home."

"Good night, Jack," she said as she kissed him on the cheek.

She walked across the road to her apartment, thinking of a nice, hot bath and an early night.

Katie was with her lawyer. She knew that as she had been with the stranger and Rita when some of his crimes were committed, if they were arrested, Katie was sure to be arrested as well. Katie asked if he thought that the courts would go easier on her if she was willing to give evidence against the stranger.

The stranger was lying awake, thinking about all the Katie knew about him and may be able to tell the police. In the morning, he told Rita that he had had an idea of how they could spend the money.

"What?" Rita said.

"Well, you know how you saw that bitch Katie in town the other day walking into a lawyer's office? Well, she may have got herself a lawyer, saying that she has evidence about you and me which could put us away for life, just to protect herself."

"Yeah, so, what has that got to do with spending the money?" Rita asked.

"Well, I've found out that the lawyer Katie saw is a woman. I thought that this afternoon, we could hang around near the solicitor's office when she is due to leave and follow her home and bribe her. I feel that she will be more likely to accept a bribe in her own home, as she would then be more 'woman' than 'lawyer.' What do you think about that?" he said excitedly.

"How much were you thinking of giving her?"

"That's not the point. Do you think it's a good idea?" the stranger asked.

"It it means we can stay together, then I'm for it."

That afternoon, they went into town and parked near the lawyer's office and waited.

"Do you know what bitch's ... I mean, Katie's lawyer looks like, or even her name?" Rita asked.

"No. I was hoping that there was just one female lawyer in that office, but I suppose we can't take that for granted."

The stranger got out of the car.

"Where are you goin'?" Rita asked.

"I'm just goin' to see what I can find out," he said and walked toward the office.

"Is Katie's lawyer in?" he asked the man at the desk.

"And you are?"

"Oh. I'm her brother, and I just want to know if her lawyer is here."

"What's the name of the lawyer?" the man asked.

"I don't know; she didn't tell me. Just said it was a woman," the stranger replied.

"Well, that narrows it down a bit." He laughed. "We only have one lady lawyer here at the moment, but she will not be able to discuss anything with you without her client's consent."

Just then, Katie's lawyer walked out from her office. She told the man at the desk that she was going home and that he could contact her on her cell phone if anything urgent arose before she reached home.

The stranger thanked the man and returned to his car and waited until the lawyer drove past in her car. He followed her at a safe distance.

She pulled up on the drive outside her house. The stranger waited for a few moments after the woman had disappeared through the front door. He wanted her to relax a bit. He pulled a sports bag containing lots of money from the truck.

The lawyer poured herself a glass of red wine, curled up in the chair, and jabbed the remote control to see if there was anything worth watching on the television before she started to prepare her evening meal. She always looked forward to unwinding this way after a stressful day at work.

Her peace was interrupted by the ringing of the doorbell. She unraveled her legs and made her way to the front door.

"Can we come in?" Rita asked.

"Who are you guys?" the lawyer said.

"We've come to talk business," the stranger replied.

"Call my office in the morning to make an appointment—"

"This can't wait!" Rita said.

"What business?"

"Let us in and I'll tell you," replied the stranger.

The lawyer stood aside and let them in. "So the business you wanted to see me about couldn't wait until the morning."

"It's about Katie," the stranger said.

"Katie who?"

"Er … Monroe, Michael, or something like that," the stranger replied.

"Oh! You mean Katie Matthews."

"Yes, that's her," the stranger said, opening the sports bag.

"What are you doing?" The lawyer stared at the bag.

"Look. I know that you have enough evidence to put me away for this life and the next, but don't you have any dreams?" the stranger said, pushing the bag over to where the lawyer was sitting.

"Are you trying to bribe me?"

"Maybe."

"How much are we talking about?" the lawyer inquired.

"For all the evidence on me and Rita, whatever you want," the stranger replied.

The lawyer just looked at the bag for a few minutes, cleared her throat, and said, "This will be between these four walls and the three of us—yes?"

The stranger nodded. She took the money and asked them to leave.

A week after the payoff, Katie went to see her lawyer to see what progress was being made.

"How's the case coming along? Do we have enough on the two bastards to put them away?"

"I've been trying to contact you about the case. I'm afraid that we don't have enough evidence to go to court. Sorry about that, but that's how it is."

"What ... but ... damn it ... thanks for nothin' ... I thought you, of all people, would have wanted to get scum like them off the streets." She stormed out of the lawyer's office.

CHAPTER 7

Katie was staying with her sister. That night, she crept into Michelle's room and quietly removed her gun from its holster. She drove around town looking for a particular black Cadillac. She spotted it about an hour later, parked outside a motel. Katie saw a light on in room number four. *Am I going to be lucky?* she thought as she knocked on the door. Her heart missed a beat when the stranger appeared.

"Remember me, asshole?" Katie said, pointing the gun in his face.

"Who is it, babe?" Rita said.

"It's our old friend, Katie," the stranger replied.

"What does she want?" Rita asked.

Katie let herself in, still pointing the gun at the stranger.

"Come on! You ain't gonna shoot me, bitch," the stranger said.

Just at the moment, the sheriff's car pulled alongside Katie's car. Michelle shouted to Katie, "No! Don't do it! Don't you want to see him rot in prison for the rest of his life? Now, drop the gun," Michelle said.

"No! I want this bastard to pay," Katie said.

"Killing him isn't going to make things better," Michelle said.

Rita got up off the bed and snatched a gun from the stranger's sports bag. She aimed it at Katie and yelled, "You shoot my guy and I'll shoot you, you fucking bitch!"

Michelle entered the motel room.

"Don't come any closer or your sister will be leaving this room in a body bag," Rita screeched.

Michelle threw her badge onto the table, which surprised Katie, and said, "Tonight, I'm above the law."

Suddenly, the stranger kicked the gun out of Katie's hand, and it slid across the floor. He kicked her hard in the abdomen and she slumped to the floor. The stranger pulled out a machine gun and was just about to shoot Katie when Michelle picked up her gun and shot him in the shoulder. He went berserk and started shooting randomly. Michelle was hit in the leg. Katie crawled to the sports bag and pulled out another gun, but as she was getting to her feet, Rita shot her in the left arm. Katie replied with bullets to Rita's chest until there were no more bullets left. Katie went to the sports bag again and this time pulled out a machine gun and then aimed it at the stranger. Michelle did the same.

"Come on, ladies; you wouldn't shoot me, would you?" the stranger asked.

"Why not?" Michelle and Katie said at the same time.

"Because I—" the stranger started.

Michelle interrupted the stranger by saying, "I'm not gonna listen to any more of your bullshit."

Then, in a heartbeat, Michelle pulled the trigger, and Katie did the same. Michelle picked up her badge from the table. They shut the door behind them as they left. A maid was just coming on duty. "This couple had a late night last night and don't want to be disturbed today," Michelle said. The two of them went to their respective cars.

"How did you find me?" Katie asked Michelle.

"I had just gone on duty when a deputy told me he had seen you driving around town."

"Thank God that's all over," Katie said in a happy voice.

"I agree with you there. Two less punks in this crazy world to deal with!" Michelle said.

Back in room number four, Rita's fingers moved.

THE END